Pete ^{the} Cat
and the Itsy Bitsy Spider

Pete the Cat and the Itsy Bitsy Spider

Library of Congress Control Number: 2018961834
ISBN 978-0-06-267544-6

The artist used pen and ink, with watercolor and acrylic paint, on
300lb hot press paper to create the illustrations for this book.
Typography by Jeanne L. Hogle
19 20 21 22 23 PC 10 9 8 7 6 5 4 3

First Edition

Pete the Cat
and the Itsy Bitsy Spider

by James Dean

HARPER

An Imprint of HarperCollinsPublishers

One day, while playing outside with his friends,
Pete the Cat spotted something cool.
"Look!" shouted Pete.

"Wow, it's so small,"
said Gus.
"It's an itsy bitsy
spider!" said Callie.

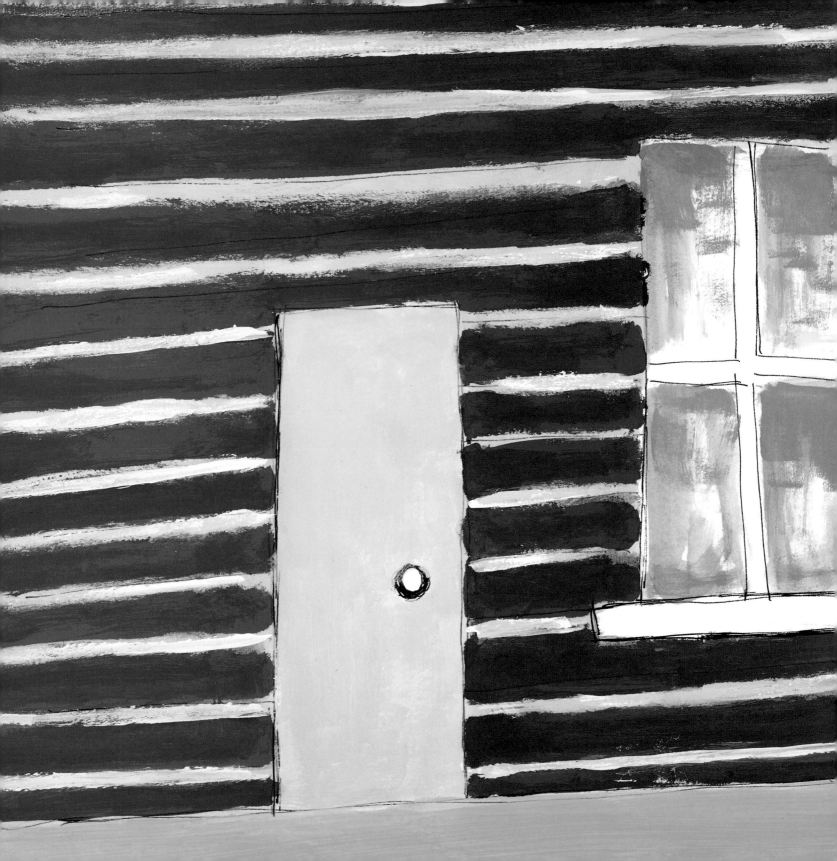

The itsy bitsy spider
climbed up the water spout.

Down came the rain
and washed the spider out.

Out came the sun
and dried up all the rain.

Pete and his friends knew just what to do.
Everyone cheered on the tiny spider.

Pete the Cat said, "Try again, itsy bitsy spider!"

So the itsy bitsy spider
climbed up the water spout.

Down came the rain
and washed the spider out.

Out came the sun
and dried up all the rain.

Pete said, "Don't give up yet!"

They all cheered louder this time.

Again the itsy bitsy spider
climbed up the water spout.

Down came the rain
and Pete and his friends shouted,

"Go, itsy bitsy spider!"

And the itsy bitsy spider
kept climbing up the water spout.

Everyone celebrated, and the spider took a bow.

With the help of some friends, the itsy bitsy spider never gave up—even when the odds were against her.